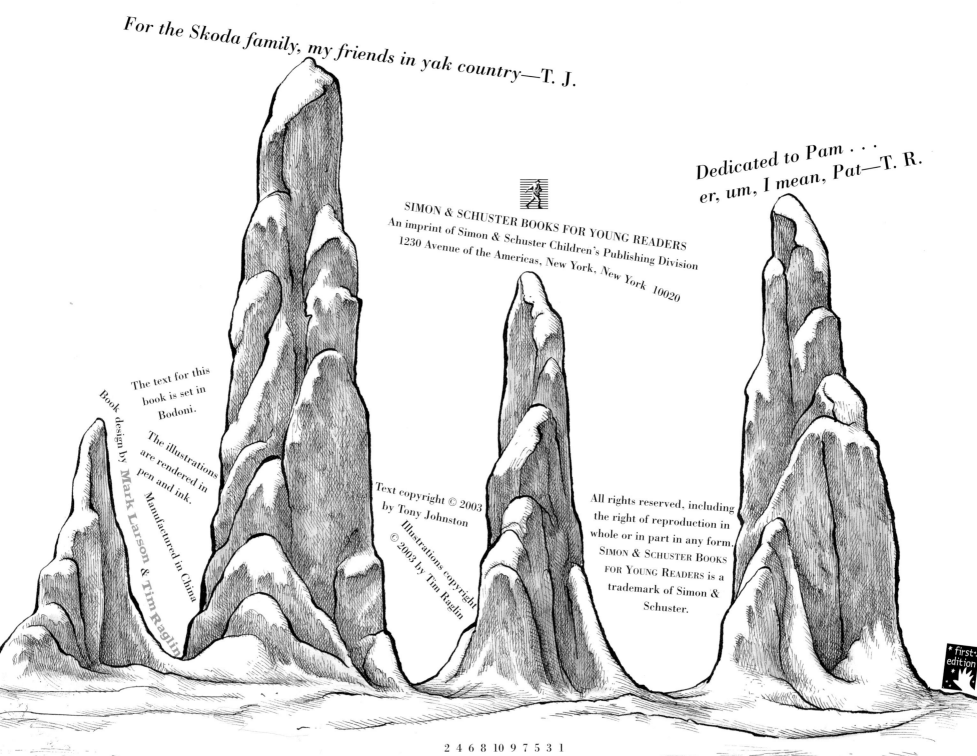

For the Skoda family, my friends in yak country—T. J.

Dedicated to Pam . . .
er, um, I mean, Pat—T. R.

SIMON & SCHUSTER BOOKS FOR YOUNG READERS
An imprint of Simon & Schuster Children's Publishing Division
1230 Avenue of the Americas, New York, New York 10020

The text for this book is set in Bodoni.

The illustrations are rendered in pen and ink.

Book design by Mark Larson & Tim Raglin

Manufactured in China

Text copyright © 2003 by Tony Johnston

Illustrations copyright © 2003 by Tim Raglin

first edition

2 4 6 8 10 9 7 5 3 1

Library of Congress Cataloging-in-Publication Data: Johnston, Tony, Go track a yak / Tony Johnston ; illustrated by Tim Raglin.—1st ed. p. cm. Summary: A couple of bumbling parents with a hungry baby seek help from a tricky little witch, but it is a sweet black-eyed yak who really helps them to live happily ever after. ISBN 0-689-83789-5 [1. Fairy tales. 2. Yak—Fiction. 3. Witches—Fiction. 4. Parents—Fiction. 5. Humorous stories.] I. Raglin, Tim, ill. II. Title. PZ8.J494 Go 2003 [E]—dc21   00-045057

GO TRACK A YAK!

By Tony Johnston   Illustrated by Tim Raglin

SIMON & SCHUSTER BOOKS FOR YOUNG READERS   New York   London   Toronto   Sydney   Singapore

Boo-hoo-hoo!

"Baby won't eat!
He'll wither away!
What shall we do?"
wailed Mama.

Boo-hoo-hoo!

Papa wailed too.
"What shall we do?"

There appeared a small crone. (A little witch, truth be known.)
"I know," she gloated, "but I'm not telling."

Boo-hoo-hoo!
Baby will wither . . .

"I'll tell the secret. If—"
she smiled slyly,
"if you promise me
my heart's desire."
(She had no heart. She was a liar.)

ANYTHING
to save our CHILD!

"Well, then, the secret is—yak juice! Only that will save the brat."

Mama and Papa stopped crying.

Then, **BOO-HOO-HOO!!**
They started again.

"Now what?" The crone grumped and stamped a foot.

We have no YAK!

The little crone SNAPPED.

Then  POOF! She vanished, just like that.

Mama crooned to the baby while Papa tracked a yak.

TREK.

TREK.

TREK.

TRACK.

TRACK.

TRACK.

Papa saw tracks,
but not from yaks.

So he sat down and sobbed.

Boo-hoo-hoo!

"Baby won't eat. He'll wither away
if I don't find a yak.
What shall I do?"

POOF!

The crone
appeared.

She sneered.
"You're such
a baby."

She turned
herself into
a crow.

"Follow me," she cawed.

Flap.
Flap.
Flap.
Track.
Track.
Track.

Up a trail so high and steep
that one false step would mean—
a BIG sleep!

But still no yak.

Then the evil crow squawked,

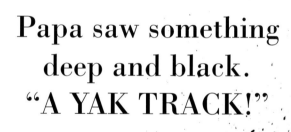

LOOK!
LOOK!
LOOK!

Papa saw something
deep and black.
"A YAK TRACK!"

POOF!

The crow vanished,
just like that.

Creep.
Creep.
Creep.
Track.
Track.
Track.

Soon, in Papa's path loomed up
the elusive, obtrusive (juice-ive) yak!

YIKES!

Papa screeched so loud that the yak stepped back and ran away.

CLOP! CLOP! CLOP!
CLACK! CLACK! CLACK!

Papa felt faint. "BOO-HOO-HOO! The baby won't eat. He'll wither away, for the yak ran off! What shall I do?"

A raspy croak came from the grass.

BAWLING and YAWLING will not catch YAKS!

POOF!

A toad stared at Papa with bulgy eyes.
(The crone, of course, in deep disguise.)
She spoke in a slurpy, burpy voice.

Come on, CRYBABY.
Follow me.
After that beast!

HOP. HOP. HOP.
Track. Track. Track.
Soon they found the runaway yak.

POOF!

The warty toad was gone.

"No more crying,"

PAPA TOLD HIMSELF.

"Think of a way
to get its juice."

Think.
Think.
Think.

Quick.
Quick.
Quick.

At last Papa made a clever list:

1. **Rope yak.**

2. **Knock yak out with rock.**

4. Lug juice home.

5. Feed Baby.

3.

Squeeze juice.

Papa braided some grass and roped the yak.

He got set to drop a rock.

But the more Papa looked
at those black yak eyes,
the more he just could not do that.

To harm
the beast
would crack
his heart.

Yet thoughts of his poor,
dear, withering baby cracked
it even more severely.

Boo-
hoo-
hoo!

"Baby won't eat.
He'll wither away,
for I can't whack the yak!
What shall I do?"

Papa was overjoyed.
He did not need to whack the yak.

Leap. Leap. Leap. Skip. Skip. Skip.

Singing, he led the yak all the way back.

Mama kissed the yak. Papa milked the yak.
And Baby gulped its milk.

Slurp.
Slurp.
Slurp.

Burp.
Burp.
Burp.

Soon Baby was
GLOWING.
And
CROWING.
Nearly
GROWING
before their
adoring eyes.

"Dear,
sweet
yak!"
said Mama
and Papa.

Goo,
Goo,
Goo!

said
Baby,
and he
hugged
the
yak.

The crone was back. She cackled. "Now for the promise you made me. Yak juice—for your baby."

Then it WALLOPED

THAT LITTLE ROTTEN CRONE.

It chucked
her
too far
to
EVER
COME
BACK.

And the little family? They never withered.
They grew fat on yak milk and yak cheese
and yak butter.

And
they lived
happily ever after.

So did the yak.

JUV
EASY
Johnst- Johnston, Tony
on
        Go track a yak!

DUE DATE

Tale of a Tiger

Written by Dugald Steer   Illustrated by Nicki Palin

Scholastic Canada Ltd.

TIKKA THE TIGER CUB lived in a rocky den, deep in the forests of India. Most nights his mother would go hunting, and most mornings she would return with food. Early one morning, when Tikka was feeling hungrier than usual, he poked his head out of the den, just to see if his mother was nearby. Outside there was a little forest clearing where Tikka would run around pretending to hunt. And right in the middle of his playground was the brightest, most colourful bird Tikka had ever seen, strutting around as if there wasn't a single tiger for a hundred miles.

IT WAS a peacock! It stood with its long tail feathers fanned out behind it in a dazzling display, while nearby a flock of peahens was pecking busily at the ground. Little Tikka was amazed. He had been feeling hungry, and here was a meal right outside his den. So just as he had seen his mother do, he crouched low and began creeping toward the bird. But no sooner had Tikka come right out of his den than – WHOOSH! The peacock and hens flapped off noisily into the trees.

TIKKA looked up toward where the peacock had gone. His little nose was twitching, and as he lifted his head to take in the smells of the waking forest, he sensed water. He knew it wasn't safe to leave the den on his own, but now that he had chased a peacock away he felt brave and strong, and he set off down to the waterhole for a drink.

As he got closer he grew even more excited. For gathered around the waterhole was a little group of monkeys, drinking and playing together. So again Tikka crouched down very low and began inching his way forward bit by bit, all the time ready to make a big leap, just like any grown-up tiger would do.

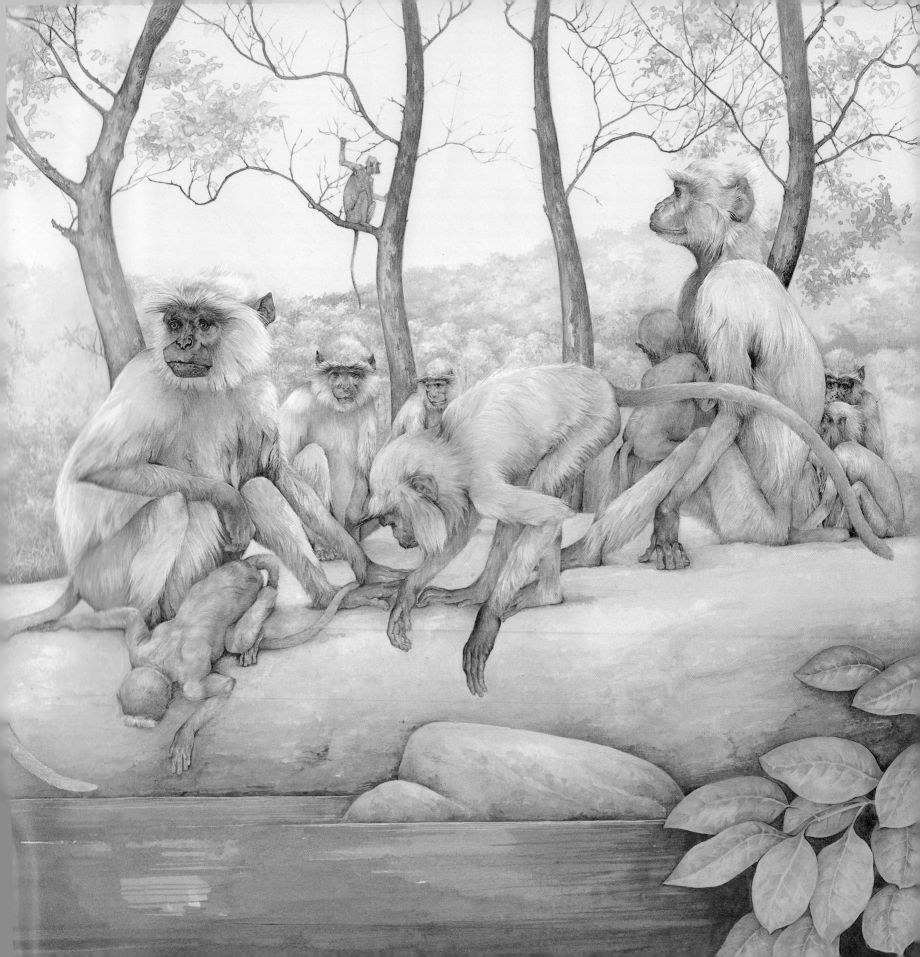

BUT THE monkeys knew all about little tiger cubs like Tikka. While the group drank and played below, one monkey sat high in a tree, looking out for trouble. He soon saw Tikka creeping around in the bushes. The lookout let out a warning cry, and at once all the other monkeys scampered up into the trees.

Tikka gave up trying to hide, had a long drink and looked around. It was time to return to the den, but he was having a wonderful adventure. What other things might await him in the forest? Why not carry on just a little farther?

TIKKA SET OFF eagerly. Soon he reached a damp gully.
It became a river during the rainy season and it
was teeming with forest life. Everywhere
Tikka looked, there were frogs and lizards,
insects and birds. But as
soon as they saw
him coming,
they fled.

The tiny frogs hopped away.

The junglefowl flapped away.

The lizards and beetles hid in
holes too small for a tiger cub's paw.
But there was one creature
who did not seem to be
bothered by Tikka at all.

IT WAS a porcupine. It felt safe, even from tigers, because it was covered in thick, sharp spines, and those spines could hurt a hungry tiger cub. Tikka snarled, just as he had seen his mother do, and the porcupine turned its back and shuffled away. It wasn't scared, but day had come and it was anxious to return to its burrow. Tikka was glad it was gone and he watched as it disappeared. He did not realize that, high above, another creature was waiting for him.

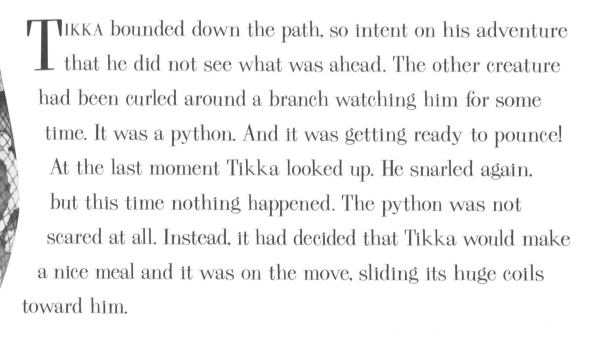

TIKKA bounded down the path, so intent on his adventure
that he did not see what was ahead. The other creature
had been curled around a branch watching him for some
time. It was a python. And it was getting ready to pounce!
At the last moment Tikka looked up. He snarled again,
but this time nothing happened. The python was not
scared at all. Instead, it had decided that Tikka would make
a nice meal and it was on the move, sliding its huge coils
toward him.

BUT JUST when everything
seemed lost, the snake's
head darted to look in another
direction. There was a fierce roar,
and Tikka's mother leaped forward
to protect him. The snake hissed
angrily but it would not fight
an adult tiger, so with a flick
of its body, it slithered away.

IT WAS lucky for Tikka that his mother had been nearby and had smelled him and heard his snarls. Now that he was safe, she led him to where she had hidden some food and he ate hungrily. Then they both padded back to the safety of their den. Tikka wouldn't leave it without his mother again until he was properly grown up. And by then there would be no forest animal that he need fear. But for now, Tikka's mother licked his ear and they both fell safely asleep.

On the Trail of a Tiger

Tigers are the world's biggest cats, growing up to 2.8 metres (9 feet) in length. They may eat up to 40 kilograms (88 pounds) of food during a single meal. There are five subspecies of tiger in the world – the Bengal, Indo-Chinese, Siberian, South Chinese and Sumatran tigers. All tigers are solitary animals that hunt by night. Each one has its own unique pattern of stripes, which helps the tiger to hide among vegetation as it stalks its prey of deer, wild pigs, monkeys, birds or reptiles. Tigers have an excellent sense of smell. Mother tigers usually give birth to two or three cubs at a time. Tigers are an endangered species, and nowadays almost all of the world's wild tigers live in protected wildlife reserves.

Tiger habitats

Tigers prefer to live in areas with plenty of cover so that they can creep up on their prey unseen. Different subspecies have made their homes everywhere from hot, humid tropical jungles to the icy forests of Siberia.

Tiger cubs

A tiger cub will stay with its mother until it is two or three years old and can hunt for its own food. The cub learns to hunt by copying its mother. A mother tiger will often leave a cub safely in a den while she goes hunting.

Peafowl

Male and female peafowl are very different in appearance. Male peafowl are called peacocks and their long tails covered in 'eyes' can be spread out like a fan. Females are smaller and less colourful. Peafowl feed on the ground, roosting in trees at night.

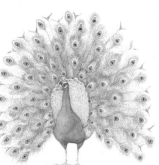

Langur monkeys

Langur monkeys live in large groups. They feed on leaves, grains and fruit and spend a lot of time each day grooming each other. When they are on the ground, sometimes one of their number stays up in a nearby tree, acting as a lookout.

Frogs and lizards

Many species of frogs and lizards live in the Indian rain forests. Lizards are good climbers, hunting insects and other small animals, while frogs often lie in wait for their prey, which can include small mice, birds or snakes. Frogs cannot chew and must swallow their food whole.

Junglefowl

Junglefowl are the ancestors of today's chickens, which were domesticated around 5,000 years ago. The male junglefowl is much bigger and more colourful than the female, with a big, red comb. Junglefowl live in groups of up to 50, and nest on the ground.

Porcupines

Porcupines have special 'rattling' spines that they use to warn potential enemies of danger. If this does not work they will turn around and charge backwards. Spines that get stuck in an animal's skin can be hard to remove and cause dangerous infections.

Pythons

Indian pythons grow up to 6 metres (20 feet) long. They kill their prey by constriction: wrapping long coils around, and then squeezing until the animal cannot breathe. They swallow their prey whole.

Tigers at risk

One hundred years ago there were more than 100,000 wild tigers in the world. Now there may be fewer than 6,000. Sixty years ago there were eight subspecies of tiger. Now there are five. As recently as 1970 it was legal to hunt tigers in India, and many thousands were killed by trophy hunters. With the rise in the human population the tiger's habitat is being destroyed. Forests are cut down to provide grazing land for farm animals, for timber, or to clear land for mining companies. The large prey that tigers need to hunt are being killed by people who need to eat themselves. And a dead tiger is worth a lot of money, either as a delicacy or for Chinese traditional medicine, so illegal hunting is big business.

For Carlos and Alberto — Dugald

First published in the UK in 2002 by Templar Publishing.
This edition published in Canada in 2003 by Scholastic Canada Ltd.
Designed by Kilnwood Graphics and Caroline Reeves

National Library of Canada Cataloguing in Publication

Steer, Dugald
Tale of a tiger / written by Dugald Steer ; illustrated by Nicki Palin.

ISBN 0-439-98956-6

1. Tiger cubs—Juvenile fiction. I. Palin, Nicki II. Title.

PZ10.3.S79Ta2003   j823'.914   C2002-901880-3

6 5 4 3 2 1   Printed in Singapore   02 03 04 05